To my nieces and nephews —
Emma, Evan, Hannah, Katie, Louis, Miriam, Ramie, and Tillie
In alphabetical order, but all first in my heart.

Big huge hugs and kisses,
Aunt Laurie

For my sweet little Juliette
J.K.

by Laurie Friedman

illustrations by Jennifer Kalis

Carolrhoda Books   Minneapolis • New York

CONTENTS

TROUBLE AVE

Pennsylvania Ave.

AN ENVELOPE FROM MR. KNIGHT

Dear Students,

Tomorrow morning we leave on our class trip to Washington, D.C. We've waited patiently for this exciting time to arrive, and at last it has!

Enclosed are several items:

Item #1: A Blank Notebook. During our trip, I expect you to keep a journal. Our nation's capital is a special place. You will all find much to write about.

When we return, you will have a week to turn in your journals. You are welcome to add in illustrations, photos, and anything else that you think will help make your journal unique. I encourage you to be creative.

Item #2: A Trip Itinerary. Enclosed are two copies of our Trip Itinerary. One is for you and the other copy is for your parents so they will be able to "go along with you" to all of the wonderful places we will be seeing.

Item #3: A class trip T-shirt. Put it on bright and early tomorrow morning. Everyone needs to be at school at 5:30! The bus leaves at 6 A.M. sharp. We don't want to leave anyone behind.
Get a good night's sleep, don't forget to pack your cameras, and get ready to have a great time in Washington, D.C.!

Sincerely,
Mr. Knight

TRIP ITINERARY

Day 1
Breakfast on bus
Arrival in Washington
White House Home of the U.S. president
Lunch
Capitol Hill Where U.S. Congress meets
Supreme Court Our nation's highest court
Library of Congress World's largest library
National Archives Home of Declaration of Independence
Dinner/Check-in
Lights out!
Day 2
Mount Vernon Home of George Washington
Lunch
Washington Monument World's tallest stone monument
Lincoln Memorial Dedicated to our 16th president
Dinner

Jefferson Memorial Nighttime viewing
Special treat!
Back to hotel
Lights out!
Day 3
National Zoo Home to many rare and exotic animals, including pandas
Early lunch (Busy afternoon!)
Smithsonian Institution The world's largest museum complex
Museum of American History
Natural History Museum
National Air and Space Museum
Dinner
Return to hotel
Lights out!
Day 4
Bureau of Engraving and Printing Printing press for U.S. stamps and all U.S. paper money
Lunch
Souvenir Shopping
Farewell Board bus
Home to Fern Falls

Mallory McDonald's Trip Journal

the JOURNEY begins HERE!

the cAPiToL

THE WHite HoUSE

Read oN

The Wheels on the Bus

ON THE BUS ON THE WAY TO W.D.C.!

Dear Trip Journal,

The wheels on the bus go around and around and around. And Mr. Knight says they have to go around a whole lot more because we have a long way to go before we get to Washington. That's the bad news.

The good news is that he's passing out doughnuts.

G.2.G.E.D. (That's short for got 2 go eat doughnuts.)

☆ Mallory

P.S. It's not so easy to write while you're on a moving bus. It's also not so easy to write when your best friend

(Mary Ann, in case you didn't know who I was talking about) is asleep on you. C B Lo 2 C what I mean.

Mallory, the human pillow

STILL ON THE BUS, STILL ON THE WAY TO W.D.C.

Dear Trip Journal,

10 things I have done since the last time I wrote in you:

#1 EATEN one plain, one chocolate, and one blueberry-filled doughnut. This sounds easy, but it wasn't because I have a loose tooth on the left side of my mouth. My friend Pamela Brooks's advice: chew the doughnuts on the right side. Also not so easy.

#2 REFUSED to be a human pillow.

#3 PLAYED Go Fish, Hearts, and Solitaire. (It is even harder to play cards on a bus than it is to write in a journal.)

#4 TRIED to pay attention while Mrs. Brooks (Pamela's mother and our official trip chaperone) read us the history of the White House. Also not so easy to do as the White House has a VERY long history, and Mrs. Brooks read us every bit of it.

#5 TALKED to lots of people on this bus including: April, Joey, Pamela, Dawn,

Zoe, Sammy, and C-Lo (a.k.a. Carlos Lopez—cute, new boy from Mexico whom I had a crush on and who I think would have had one back on me except that Mary Ann claimed him first). I didn't actually talk to him. Mary Ann did. But I sat next to her while she did.

Note to viewer: MUCH CUTER in real life

#6 GONE to the bathroom (4 times). How cool is it that there is a bathroom on this bus?

#7 READ three magazines.

#8 FILLED OUT one magazine questionnaire (with Mary Ann) about finding your soul mate. According to our answers, hers is right here on this bus and mine is in Australia.

#9 TAKEN pictures of people on the bus. Most of the people were awake and smiling (like Pamela), but some were asleep and snoring (like Joey). Here's a fact: Awake and smiling people look better in pictures than asleep and snoring ones. (I'm leaving a space to put in pictures so you can see what I mean.)

AWAKE vs ASLEEP? U DECIDE!

#10 LISTENED to Max's iPod, which I still can't believe he let me bring on this trip. (Note to self: Buy nice gift for Max so he will let me borrow iPod more often.)

I just asked Mr. Knight if we are almost there. He didn't answer, which I think means we still have a long way to go.

☆ Mallory

P.S. Actually, I did 11 things since the last time I wrote in you.

#11 WIGGLED my loose tooth (a lot). On a scale of 1-10, Pamela said my tooth is a 4, which means I have a lot more wiggling to do.

G.2.G. (Got to go.) G.2.W. (Got to wiggle!)
☆ Mallory

STILL ON THE BUS,
STILL ON THE WAY TO W.D.C.

Dear Trip Journal,

This bus ride is taking a looooong time, which means I have had a loooong time to think about something that is bothering me. And that something is that I don't really like writing *Dear Trip Journal*. If you ask me, writing *Dear Trip Journal* sounds kind of grownup-ish, and not so cute, if you know what I mean.

So ... I've decided I'm going to name you. I have a very nice name picked out, but before I tell you, I want to tell Mary Ann. So B.R.B.A.S.A.I.T.M.A. (That's short for be right back as soon as I tell Mary Ann.)

☆ ☆ ☆ ☆ ☆ ☆ ☆

OK. I'm back. Mary Ann loved the name I picked. It's Martha! As in Martha

Washington. George's wife. Get it? Love it?!?
I hope so because it's yours! From now on,
I'm going to be writing *Dear Martha* instead
of *Dear Trip Journal.*
☆ *Mallory*

P.S. Mary Ann is going to call
her trip journal Zac Efron.

STILL ON THE BUS,
STILL ON THE WAY TO W.D.C.

Dear Martha,
Mr. Knight said we're getting close!
He also said he has some rules he wants
to go over, AND he's going to tell us who
our partners will be when we go places
and whom we will be rooming with at the
hotel. Pamela just told me it's time to stop
writing and start paying attention.
☆ *Mallory*

STILL ON THE BUS, STILL ON THE WAY TO (You guessed it!) W.D.C.

Dear Martha,

Mr. Knight just gave out the rules we're supposed to follow:

Mr. Knight's List of Rules

Rule #1: Don't wander off.

Rule #2: Stick with the group.

Rule #3: Stay alert and focused.

Rule #4: Stay with your partner.

Rule #5: NO sightseeing on your own.

Joey just said he's not sure why Mr. Knight gave us all those rules, because in his opinion, they all mean the same thing, which is DON'T GET LOST!

Pamela said Mr. Knight is just trying to emphasize a V.I.P. (short for a Very Important Point).

Mr. Knight also gave out partner assignments and room assignments. My

PAMELA BROOKS
S.S.F.
(SUPER SMART FRIEND)

partner assignment is all good. It's Mary Ann. When we found out, Mary Ann said: "YEAH! YEAH! YEAH!"

My room assignment is half good and half bad. (NO YEAH! YEAH! YEAH!)

C chart 2 C what I mean.

ROOM ASSIGNMENTS

THE GOOD HALF = MARY ANN

THE BAD HALF = ARIELLE & DANIELLE

If you're wondering why I think sharing a room with Arielle and Danielle for the next four days will be bad, I will give you an example.

Right when Mr. Knight announced the room assignments, Danielle tapped Mary Ann on the shoulder and said, "Arielle and I get first dibs on the bathroom."

Then Arielle looked at me and said, "Danielle and I call the closet."

Martha, if you were a wish pond (like the one on my street), I would make a wish, and the wish I would make is that living with Arielle and Danielle for the next four days won't be as bad as I think it will be.
☆ *Mallory*

P.S. Mr. Knight just said we are getting close.

STILL ON THE BUS, BUT NOT FOR MUCH LONGER!

Dear Martha,

Mr. Knight just announced that we are in Alexandria, Virginia!!! This time, I was the one who said, "YEAH! YEAH! YEAH!"

You're probably wondering why I'm so excited to be in Alexandria, and the reason is because Mr. Knight also said that Alexandria is a hop, skip, and a jump away from Washington.

Translation: We are very close and everyone on this bus is very excited!

☆ Mallory

STILL ON THE BUS, BUT GETTING READY TO GET OFF!

Martha,

Mr. Knight just said to pack up our belongings and to dispose of our trash in the bag as he walks through the aisles. Right now, he sounds more like a flight attendant (or in this case, a bus attendant) than he does a teacher.

But I don't care ... because guess what ... we're here! It's time to get off this bus!

☆ Mallory

One more thing: Here's a We-Arrived poem!

YEAH! YEAH! YEAH!
YIPPEE! YIPPEE! YIPPEE!
I never thought we'd get here,
But we're in WASHINGTON, D.C.!

NOTE TO MR. KNIGHT:
   I didn't actually make up this poem. Mary Ann did. But she said it would be super cute if we both put it in our journals. Also, if you get sick of being a teacher, you would make a good bus attendant.
   ☆ Mallory

We're in Washington!

IN WASHINGTON, D.C., AT THE WHITE HOUSE

Dear Martha,

You're never going to believe where I am! If you guessed 1600 Pennsylvania Avenue, then you guessed right. I'm standing in front of the house of the president of the United States of America! His house is not only very big, but it's also very white.

Here's what everyone said when we got off the bus:

Mary Ann: Wow! Wow! Wow! White! White! White!

Joey: They must have used up all the white paint when they built this place.

Pamela: I want to take some pictures.

Mrs. Brooks: Hurry up! Our official tour
is about to begin.

I say no time 2 write now. I want 2
take some pictures, and then I want 2
see where the president of the United
States lives!

More later!

☆ Mallory

AT THE WHITE HOUSE VISITOR CENTER

Dear Martha,

We just finished our tour of the White
House. There are a lot of things I learned.

Some of the things I learned from
Henry, our tour guide, but most things I
learned from Mrs. Brooks.

Whenever Henry would say something
like, "This is the official State Dining Room

where all of the important dinners at the White House are held," Mrs. Brooks would say something like, "Let me just add that this room seats as many as 140 people."

Henry gave Mrs. Brooks lots of *I'm-the-tour-guide-so-I'll-do-the-talking* looks. But Mrs. Brooks was too busy talking to notice.

Also, a couple of times, kids in my class gave Mrs. Brooks *TMI* looks. But I don't think Mrs. Brooks noticed those looks either.

TMI = Too much information

I have to stop writing about Mrs. Brooks and start making a list of what I thought were the most interesting things we learned about the White House. Mr. Knight says everybody has to do it because that way we'll remember more

about all of the places we're going to see.
He also said no one gets lunch until we do.

☆ Mallory

Mallory McDonald's List of Interesting Things about the White House

THING #1: Rooms in the White House come in lots of colors. We saw a red one, a blue one, and a green one.

THING #2: The rooms in the White House are very big, especially the East Room. It's the biggest room of all, and it's been used for lots of things, including

weddings, funerals, famous speeches, a high school prom, and to hang up the president's wet laundry. (Pamela said that must have happened before dryers were invented.)

THING #3: There are some rooms in the White House that you can't see, like the Oval Office. That's where the president does his official business (and I don't mean the kind you do in a bathroom).

THING #4: You are NOT allowed to use the bathroom in the White House (even though there are over 30 of them!). I know because I asked Henry if I could use the bathroom. He said I was not allowed. Then Arielle, Danielle, April, Dawn, and Brittany all asked if they could. Henry said NO ONE is allowed to use the bathroom in the White House.

So I asked if the president is allowed to use the bathroom in the White House. Lots of people (all under the age of 10) thought that was very funny. But other people (all over the age of 10, and including anyone named Mr. Knight, Mrs. Brooks, and Henry) did not.

OK. That's what I learned at the White House. Also, I bought a bunch of postcards at the Visitor Center.

I would write one to Mom, Dad, Max, and Cheeseburger, but Mr. Knight says it's time for lunch, which is a good thing because Pete, Sammy, and Zack are all having a *who's-stomach-is-rumbling-the-loudest* contest.

After lunch, we're off to Capitol Hill to see the Capitol, the Supreme Court, the Library of Congress, and the National Archives. I don't know what exactly we're going to see in all those places, but I know I can't wait to see it.

☆ Mallory

Liberty and JUSTICE ☆ for all

Me with Pamela at the U.S. Capitol

MAP

SUPREME COURT

LIBRARY OF CONGRESS

U.S. Capitol

capitol

HIll

Rights and Wrongs

AFTER LUNCH

Dear Martha,

I have a stomach problem ... mine is empty. We had what Mrs. Brooks said was an "all-American" lunch. Hot dogs and hamburgers. Aside from being all-American, it also happens to be my favorite lunch, but I couldn't eat it.

I tried to eat my hot dog, but it was too hard to do with a loose tooth. Pamela said I should do the same thing with the hot dog that I did with the doughnut, which was chew it on my right side.

I tried, but while I was busy right-side chewing, other people were busy making fun of me.

MALLORY'S OVERSIZED CHEEK

Arielle: Mallory, what do you have in your right cheek, a peach?

Danielle: It looks more like a tennis ball.

Pete: Is there a water balloon in there?

April: Maybe it's a mattress.

Zack: It might be the District of Columbia.

In case you don't know what the District of Columbia is, it's the D.C. part of Washington. According to Mrs. Brooks, the Founding Fathers of our country decided to put the nation's capital in its own district so no one state could say it belonged to them.

So what's the moral of the story? If you said that our Founding Fathers were fair people, you are wrong.

The moral of the story is that nobody can eat lunch when somebody says it looks like you're eating our nation's capital (especially when you're at the nation's capital). So now, I am starving!

☆ Mallory

P.S. In case you're wondering why my best friend (still Mary Ann, but I'm starting to wonder) didn't protect me while everybody was making fun of me, it's because she was too busy sharing her lunch with C-LO.

Turn page 2 C what I mean.

ON THE STEPS OF THE CAPITOL

Dear Martha,

We just took a tour of the United States Capitol, which is where all the laws in our country get made. While we were on our tour, Jackson said he thinks it would be a really bad idea to break a law while you're at the Capitol, and Mrs. Brooks said it is ALWAYS a bad idea to break a law ... no matter where you are.

She also said that visiting the Capitol was a perfect time for a spelling lesson. I don't think anybody wanted a spelling lesson, but she gave one anyway. She said that the building we just toured is spelled C-A-P-I-T-O-L. But the city (Washington, D.C.) we are visiting is spelled C-A-P-I-T-A-L.

Mr. Knight says it's time to write down a little bit about the Capitol before we move on to the Supreme Court. So here goes:

Mallory McDonald's List of Interesting Things about the Capitol

THING #1: The Capitol is where the United States House of Representatives and the United States Senate (together a.k.a. Congress) meet to work, and we got to watch them while they were in session. Something I learned about the men and women who work in Congress is that they seem very polite. While we were there, if one person was talking and someone else wanted to say something, they just raised their hand and asked the person in charge if they could have a turn. Arielle said she can't imagine that they're always polite. Danielle said no one is always polite. I think some people (I don't want to say any names, but here's a hint: their names start with an "A" and a "D," I'm going to

42

be sharing a hotel room with them) are almost never polite. But Mr. Knight said Congress has rules for behavior just like we have classroom rules.

THING #2: The Rotunda is the big round thing on the top of the Capitol. It is 180 feet high and 96 feet wide. It has more than 800 pieces of artwork in it. When I get home, I'm going to ask Dad if we can add a rotunda to my room.

My New Bedroom

THING #3: The Capitol makes people get in trouble (though fortunately, not me). When we were at the Capitol, we saw lots of statues of famous people. Mrs. Brooks said they were all important people like politicians, historians, and even astronauts. Pete (a kid in my class) asked Mrs. Brooks if any of the statues were chaperones on school field trips. I thought it was a good question, but apparently Mr. Knight did not because he told Pete not to be a wise guy. Pete said he was trying to get wise by asking questions, and that's when he got in trouble.

OK. That's what I learned at the Capitol. Now we're going to see the Supreme Court, the Library of Congress, and the National Archives. Then we get to stop for ice cream. Hopefully there won't be a lot to see at the places I just mentioned, because I can't wait to stop for ice cream.

☆ Mallory

SITTING ON THE GRASS NEXT TO AN ICE CREAM TRUCK

Dear Martha,

We did a LOT of sightseeing this afternoon and a LITTLE bit of ice cream eating. We all got to pick one thing. (I thought I should have gotten two since I didn't eat my lunch, but Mr. Knight did not agree.) Joey, Pamela,

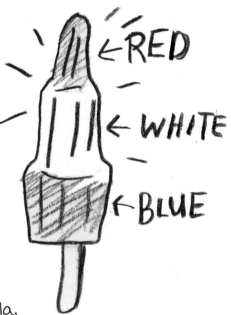

← RED

← WHITE

← BLUE

and I picked red, white, and blue Popsicles, which Mr. Knight said was a very patriotic thing to do.

Here's another thing Mr. Knight said this afternoon (and he said it everywhere we went): STICK WITH YOUR PARTNER!

I tried to stick with mine (Mary Ann), but to tell you the truth, I thought she was trying a lot harder to stick with C-Lo than she was with me.

No time to write about B.B.F.B. (that's short for bad best friend behavior) now. Time to write down my "interesting facts" from the places we saw because Mr. Knight says that when everyone is finished, we are going to get back on the bus and go check in to our hotel. YEAH! I CAN'T WAIT TO CHECK OUT OUR HOTEL!

☆ Mallory

Mallory McDonald's List of Interesting Things about the Supreme Court, the Library of Congress, and the National Archives

THING #1: The Supreme Court is the most important court in all the land. (Mrs. Brooks's words, not mine.) It also has a cute nickname: The Marble Palace. I wouldn't be surprised if there wasn't any marble left after the Supreme Court was built. There are 16 marble columns in front (Joey counted and told me) and a 5-story marble staircase inside.

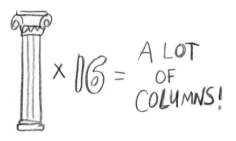

$\times 16 =$ A LOT OF COLUMNS!

In case you're wondering what marble is, I'll tell you. It's fancy white stone and it's everywhere at that place.

THING #2: A lot of judges work at the Supreme Court. They are called justices. There's one head judge and eight not-head judges. Pete said (and Joey and I both agreed) it would be a lot more interesting if there was one judge with eight heads.

GUINNESS WORLD RECORD?
JUDGE WITH THE MOST HEADS.

LOTS OF
BOOKS!

THING #3: The Library of Congress is the biggest library in the world. Mrs. Brooks provided us with many "interesting facts" (her words, not mine) while we were there. For example, she said there are over 29 million books in the library.

THING #4: There are lots of places to buy coffee at the Library of Congress. Pete said it's because people get sleepy when they read so they need coffee to stay awake. Joey said people also get sleepy on tours.

THING #5: Balloons are not the only place to put helium. At the National Archives, we saw our nation's most important documents: the Constitution, the Bill of Rights, and the Declaration of Independence. And guess what? They're all in a case filled with helium, which Pamela said helps keep them fresh. Cool, huh!

HELIUM

THING #6: The Bill of Rights is one of the most important documents ever written. That is what our tour guide, Selma, told us when we were at the National Archives.

Selma: The Bill of Rights is important because it limits the powers of the government and protects the rights of citizens.

Right when she started telling us about some of those rights, like freedom of speech

and press and religion, I started wiggling
my loose tooth. Mr. Knight told me to stop
wiggling and pay attention. He said it is
very important to understand our rights as
citizens.

In case you weren't sure, I agree with Mr.
Knight that it is important to understand
our rights as citizens. I think all citizens
should have the right to wiggle a loose tooth.

MY RIGHT TO WIGGLE!

What I don't think citizens (Mary Ann) should have the right to do is sit next to someone on the bus (C-Lo) who is not their partner. That's what Mary Ann is doing right now, and I think it's "wrong."

Well, it's my right to sit wherever I want, and I'm going to sit next to Pamela.

☆ Mallory

P.S. We're at the hotel!

Lights Out

IN THE HOTEL ROOM, ALMOST BEDTIME

Dear Martha,

I'm in my hotel room (which is also Mary Ann's and Arielle's and Danielle's hotel room). Mrs. Brooks just knocked on our door and told us 10 minutes until

PORTRAIT OF A GRUMPY CHAPERONE

lights out. She said that it is time to turn off the TV, brush our teeth, and write in our journals. She said when she comes back in 10 minutes, it will be lights out and mouths shut time. And to be honest, she didn't say any of it in a very nice voice.

A lot has happened since we checked in to this hotel. Some of it has been good, but some of it has been not-so good.

I'll tell you the good things first.

GOOD THING #1: This hotel is a very cool place. All of the rooms are named after United States presidents and decorated to look like the time when that person was president. Our room is the Bill Clinton room. There are pictures of Bill and Hillary and their daughter, Chelsea, all over the room. Also, there are very cute, little bottles of shampoo and conditioner and miniature soaps in the bathroom. Arielle and Danielle said when they get home, they're going to ask their moms if they can start getting these.

SOAP VS. CHOCOLATES = NO CONTEST

GOOD THING #2: This hotel is a very yummy place. There were chocolates shaped like American flags on all the pillows. Mmmm! When Mary Ann and I get home, we're going to ask our moms if we can start getting these.

GOOD THING #3: Mary Ann and I wore our matching American flag pajamas,

YOU LOOK CUTE!

and we looked very cute wearing them. Even Arielle and Danielle (who never say anything nice) said we did.

OK. Now it's time for the not-so-good things, which all happened to me because of one not-so-good person, and that person is Mary Ann.

NOT-SO-GOOD THING #1: Right when we got to our room, Arielle and Danielle said, "We get the closet." I said, "No fair!" Then I looked at Mary Ann because that's when she was supposed to say, "No fair!" too. But she didn't. All she said to Arielle and Danielle was, "You can have the closet." What she said to me was, "Don't you think C-Lo has nice eyes?" I couldn't believe Mary Ann was thinking about C-Lo's eyes when what she should have been thinking about was where we were going to put our stuff.

NOT-SO-GOOD THING #2: After dinner, Mr. Knight said everyone could watch

a little bit of TV in our rooms. So I said
to Arielle and Danielle, "Mary Ann and
I get to pick the show since you picked
the closet." I gave Mary Ann a tell-'em-
that's-how-it's-going-to-work look. But
Mary Ann didn't do that. All she said was
that she didn't care what we watched
because she wanted to straighten her
hair. Then she asked me if I thought
C-Lo would like her with straight hair.

NOT-SO-GOOD THING #3: When I
went into the bathroom to wiggle my

tooth, I asked Mary Ann three times
if she wanted to see my loose tooth,
and all she said was that she was busy
straightening her hair.

And Mary Ann wasn't the only one
who didn't want to see my tooth. Arielle
and Danielle didn't want to see it either.
(They were too busy watching the show
Mary Ann let them pick.)
☆ Mallory

STILL IN THE HOTEL ROOM, BEDTIME

Dear Martha,

Mrs. Brooks just knocked on our door
and said, "Lights out!"

Except for the fact that I had to
deal with a tooth and a friend who both
misbehaved, today was a lot of fun. I
can't wait for tomorrow to get here.

Good night, sleep tight, and don't let the bedbugs bite (though to be honest with you, if they take a little nibble out of Mary Ann, it's just fine with me).

☾☆ Mallory

Partner Problems

AT THE HOTEL,
AT THE COFFEE SHOP

Dear Martha,

We're at the hotel eating breakfast at what Mr. Knight said is a coffee shop. I don't know why they call it a coffee shop when coffee is the most boring thing on the menu. There's lots of great stuff here like eggs, bacon, and cinnamon rolls. That's why Mary Ann, Pamela, and I decided they

WHY DRINK THIS?

WHEN YOU CAN HAVE THIS!

should call this place the egg, bacon, and cinnamon roll shop.

In case you're wondering if we enjoyed our breakfast, here's the answer. Pamela and Mary Ann enjoyed theirs. Mine tasted great, but I didn't enjoy it because of something that happened.

After we got our food, Mary Ann, Pamela, April, and I sat down together. We were about to start eating when C-Lo walked over to our table. Then here's what happened:

C-LO: (big smile) Mary Ann, I was wishing to eat breakfast with you.

Mary Ann: (even bigger smile) What a great idea!

C-LO: (big frown) But there is no room at this table for me.

What Mary Ann said: No problem. I'll just move.

What I thought she should have said:
  Sorry, I'm having breakfast with my
  best friend!!!
What C-LO did: (stopped frowning,
  started smiling)
  Martha, Mary Ann just picked up her
plate and went and sat at another table
with C-LO. She didn't even say *bye*.
Now do you see why I didn't enjoy my
breakfast?
     ☹ *Mallory*

  P.S. Another reason breakfast was hard
to enjoy was because of the whole tooth
thing. I wiggled it for Pamela, and she said
she thinks it got looser while I was sleeping.

  P.P.S. I asked Joey if he thought the
whole Mary Ann and C-Lo thing was a little
weird and he said he hadn't even thought

about it. But he said he had
thought about my tooth and
he would be happy to yank it
out for me. I told him no one
is yanking anything.

$6\frac{1}{2}$ on Loose
TOOTH SCALE

    P.P.P.S. We're going to Mount Vernon
this morning. It was George Washington's
house, which means it's really old because
he was the first president of our country
and there have been
42 of them since
him. If you're
wondering how I
know the exact
number of
presidents, the
answer (you
guesssed it) is
Mrs. Brooks.

AMERICA'S FIRST
PRESIDENT

AT MOUNT VERNON, OUTSIDE THE BATHROOM

Dear Martha,

I only have a minute to tell you this because our tour of Mount Vernon is about to begin, but something AWFUL, AWFUL, AWFUL happened to me in the bathroom and then something even more AWFUL, AWFUL, AWFUL happened when I came out of the bathroom.

I was in the bathroom with April, Dawn, Pamela, Mary Ann, and Zoe. And Martha, I don't know if you know this, but going to the bathroom on a field trip with all of your friends should be one of the best parts of a field trip, only it wasn't for me. Keep reading and you will see why.

AN AWFUL THING

STAY TUNED

When I opened my mouth to show my friends my loose tooth (sorry to keep bringing up the whole tooth thing, but when you hear what happened next, you'll see why I had to mention it), Mary Ann walked out of the bathroom. That's right! She walked out right in the middle of the show!

When I went outside, she was sitting on a ledge talking to (guess who ... if you guessed C-Lo, you guessed right)! Then Mr. Knight told everyone to get with their partner. Well, guess what (again)? Mary Ann didn't move to get with me!

Martha, do you know what this means? It means my best friend would rather sit on a ledge and talk to a boy than be partners with me.

I'm starting to think I have a partner problem.

☹ Mallory

STILL AT MOUNT VERNON

Dear Martha,

We spent the whole morning touring Mount Vernon.

What I got to see:

The house where George Washington lived, a museum with all his stuff, and a movie about George Washington's life.

What I didn't get to see:

Mary Ann. I know she was here because every time C-Lo said something, she laughed really loud (too loud, if you

KNOCK IT OFF!

ask me). I also know Mrs. Brooks thought she was laughing too loud because I heard her say to Mary Ann, "I'm glad to see you're enjoying

Mount Vernon, but perhaps you can voice your enthusiasm a little more quietly."

OK. Mr. Knight just said we have to write down what we thought was interesting about this place. Here's my list:

Mallory McDonald's List of Interesting Things about Mount Vernon

THING #1: Mount Vernon isn't actually in Washington, D.C. It's 16 miles outside of Washington, D.C., in the state of Virginia. That means that we had to take a field trip on our field trip just to see it, but I was glad to do it because a) I love field trips (except when friends don't exhibit appropriate field-trip behavior. You know what I'm talking about!) and b) we saw lots of cool stuff at Mount Vernon.

THING #2: George Washington lived

at Mount Vernon for 45 years. He lived there from the time he was 22 until his death. That means he lived at Mount Vernon even longer than I've lived on Wish Pond Road.

I CANNOT TELL A LIE!

THING #3: There are a lot of wax heads at Mount Vernon. You can see George when he was 19, 45, and 57. When I get home, I'm going to make a wax head of Cheeseburger.

THING #4: There are a lot of trees at Mount Vernon, even though George was famous for chopping them down.

THING #5: When you go in the mansion, you can see the bed that George Washington slept in. When we saw it, Joey said, "Wow! That is a really old bed."

And that made me think about bedbugs (who like old beds), which made me think about how when Mary Ann and I have sleepovers, we always say to each other, "Good night, sleep tight, don't let the bedbugs bite." And then, I started thinking about Mary Ann, who I know was thinking about C-Lo and not me or bedbugs or sleepovers. So I said to myself, "Stop thinking about bedbugs and sleepovers and Mary Ann right this instant!" And I haven't thought about any of it since (except for now when I wrote about it).

OK. That's my list of interesting things. I thought it was all very interesting, except for the parts about Mary Ann and C-Lo. I know it seems like it bothers me that she is spending a lot of time with him, but it doesn't. Not at all. OK. Maybe just a little.

☹ Mallory

M Is for Monuments

AT THE WASHINGTON MONUMENT

Dear Martha,

We just ate lunch at a food court.

Pamela, April, Zack, and I had Chinese food.

Joey and Pete got chicken fingers and

WHAT I ATE

french fries. Arielle, Danielle, Brittany, and Dawn bought pretzels and milk shakes. Emma and Evan tried Middle Eastern food. And guess who had Mexican food?

If you guessed Mary Ann, then you guessed right. If you guessed that the reason she picked Mexican is because C-Lo thought it would be fun for them to

eat the food from his country together . . .
right again!

WHAT MARY ANN ATE

When I asked Mary Ann if she wanted
to get Chinese food with me, she said,
"Maybe some other time." Then she

went and stood
with C-Lo in the
Mexican food
line. Martha,
Mary Ann and
I have always
done everything

THE NEW MALLORY?

together. I feel like C-Lo is becoming the new Mallory.

Another 🙁, *Mallory*

P.S. We're about to go up to the top of the Washington Monument. T.T.U.W.I.C.B.D. (Talk to U When I Come Back Down), which might be a while because, as Joey just pointed out, the Washington Monument is veeeeeeeeeeeeeeeeeeeeeeeeeeeeeeeeeeeeery tall!

STILL AT THE WASHINGTON MONUMENT

Dear Martha,

I'm back down and I have a few interesting things to tell you about the monument dedicated to the first president of our country.

Mallory McDonald's List of Interesting Things about the Washington Monument

THING #1: Joey was right about this place being tall. Mrs. Brooks told me that the Washington Monument is exactly 555 feet tall.

If you're wondering how tall that is, I'll give you a comparison. I'm 4 feet and 6 inches tall.

BIG MONUMENT

Little Me

THING #2: This place
is surrounded by flags.
Fifty of them, to be exact.
There's one American flag
to represent each of the 50
states. When April saw them, she told
Mr. Knight that it was a good thing there
aren't 3,000 states because that would
be a LOT of flags. Mr. Knight said he is
always amazed by April's observations.

THING #3: It took almost 30 years to
build the Washington Monument (which
is even longer than it takes my brother,
Max, to finish a book report).

THING #4: The view from the top of the
Washington Monument is AWESOME! It's
like being in an airplane. You can see all of
Washington, D.C. Joey, Pamela, and I took
lots of pictures. I can't wait to show them
to Mom and Dad and Max so they can see

how high up I was.

THING #5: While I was at the top of the Washington Monument, I was so busy looking around, I forgot about my tooth. But as

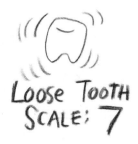

Loose Tooth
Scale: 7

soon as I got back down, I remembered it, and so did Pamela. We decided it is definitely looser this afternoon than it was this morning.

The other thing I remembered when I got back down is Mary Ann. I hadn't actually forgotten her (more like she had forgotten me). But when we got down, Mr. Knight reminded us all to get with our partners, and Mary Ann got with me like she'd never really left. Maybe she got sick of C-Lo (or just ate too many tortilla chips). Whatever, I'm glad she's back to being my partner and I hope she stays my partner.

OK. We're about to leave this monument and go to another one. Actually, the one we're going to is a memorial. I know because Mrs. Brooks just looked over my shoulder and when she saw that I had written *monument*, she said that what we will be seeing is technically a *memorial.*

☆ *Mallory*

MONUMENT   -vs.-   MEMORIAL   THE SAME thing if you ask me

AT THE LINCOLN MEMORIAL

Dear Martha,

The memorial we just saw is the Lincoln Memorial, and I'm going to tell you really quickly what I thought was interesting about it because as soon as everyone is done, we're having what Mr. Knight calls a fruit-filled afternoon.

We're going to eat fruit (a.k.a. Apple Pie! Mmmm!).

☆ Mallory

Mallory McDonald's List of Interesting Things about the Lincoln Memorial

THING #1: Mr. Lincoln was one of the most important presidents of the United States. He was president during

YEAH FOR MR. LINCOLN!

the Civil War, which was when our country was split in half because some people believed in slavery and some people did not. Mr. Lincoln did not and since he was president, he made everybody get rid of it.

THING #2: There's a really BIG statue of Mr. Lincoln inside his memorial. When Pete saw the statue, he said that if Mr. Lincloln was this big, it's a shame he was

NOTE: ACTUAL STATUE MUCH BIGGER!

president and not a basketball player.

THING #3: I bought a really pretty postcard of the Lincoln Memorial. C.B.L.2.C.W.I.M. (C B L0 2 see what I mean.)

OK. That's it. Time to get fruity!

♡ Mallory

AT THE PIE PLACE

Dear Martha,

Mr. Knight wasn't kidding about us having a fruit-filled afternoon.

I would also call it a fun-filled afternoon. We just ate apple pie. Everybody LOVED it!

It was hot and fresh out of the oven. Danielle said it smelled better than her new perfume, and for once, I agreed with Danielle.

Pamela couldn't eat all of hers, so she let me finish it.

Also, Mary Ann stayed with me the whole time. This afternoon was AWESOME.

Tonight, Mr. Knight says he has a night planned that we will always remember.

If it's half as much fun as our afternoon,

I can't wait!

☆ Mallory

THIS STUFF TASTES AND SMELLS G-R-E-A-T!

UNforGEttaBLe!

Pamela and me
with
Mr. Jefferson

Joey, capital city
Ice cream Eating
champion

A Night to Remember

Dear Martha,

Tonight we went to see the Jefferson Memorial, which, as Mr. Knight said, is a memorial to the third president of the United States who was a very important author. He wrote the Declaration of Independence, which Mrs. Brooks said is

WHICH WOULD YOU RATHER READ?

even more important than the last Harry Potter book, though I'm not so sure I agree with her.

Then we went to get banana splits.

Before we went, Mr. Knight said tonight would be a night we will always remember. And boy was he right. I will ALWAYS remember what happened tonight.

Actually, a lot of people said they will ALWAYS remember tonight too.

Pamela said she will ALWAYS remember seeing the Jefferson Memorial lit up.

Pete said he will ALWAYS remember seeing the statue of Thomas Jefferson inside the memorial.

Joey said he will ALWAYS remember tonight because he ate a whole banana split (one scoop of chocolate ice cream with marshmallow topping, one scoop of strawberry ice cream with caramel sauce,

WARNING! EAT AT YOUR OWN RISK!

and one scoop of cookies and cream ice cream with hot fudge) in under 2 minutes. Zack dared him to do it, so he did, but he said he'll ALWAYS remember tonight because eating all that ice cream so fast gave him a bad stomachache.

But none of them will remember tonight for the same reason as me. I will ALWAYS remember tonight because ... C-Lo asked Mary Ann to be his girlfriend, and she said YES!

Martha, I don't get it.

BOO! BAD ANSWER

First of all, I don't know why C-Lo asked Mary Ann to be his girlfriend. He's on a field trip to Washington, D.C., and he's supposed to be paying attention to our nation's capital, NOT to Mary Ann.

Second of all, I don't get why Mary Ann said she would be his girlfriend. She should be paying attention to what we're seeing on this field trip too. And I think she's too young to be a girlfriend. Plus, we're best friends, and I think best friends should talk about becoming a girlfriend before they just become one.

It's like Mary Ann and C-Lo are both totally missing the point of this trip, and Mary Ann is totally missing the point of being a best friend.

This whole thing is giving me a giant headache (mainly because Mary Ann has been screeching in my ear all night).

And even though we're back at the hotel and in bed and we're supposed to be "quieting down," Mary Ann is still screeching.

I'm going to the bathroom to wiggle my tooth one more time, and then I'm going to bed.

☾☆ Mallory

P.S. When I went to wiggle my tooth, I came back from the bathroom and told Mary Ann that I feel different tonight than I did this morning because my tooth

is even looser now than it was when I
woke up. And guess what Mary Ann said
to me!?! She said she knows exactly how
I feel because she feels different tonight
than she did this morning, because when
she woke up this morning she wasn't a
girlfriend and now she is.

P.P.S. Arielle and Danielle just said
they've heard enough about my tooth
but not nearly enough about C-Lo. And

right now, they're sitting on my bed
listening to Mary Ann go blah, blah, blah
about C-Lo. Martha, I know you'll agree
with me that a loose tooth is a lot more
interesting than some stupid boyfriend!

Letter to a Panda

ON THE BUS ON THE WAY TO THE ZOO

Dear Martha,

We just ate breakfast and we're on our way to the National Zoo. But guess what?

Some of us did not eat breakfast. To be exact, one of us did not eat breakfast and that one of us is Mary Ann. She said she couldn't think about eating because all she can think about is C-Lo.

I, personally, don't see what thinking about C-Lo has to do with eating breakfast.

I told Mary Ann that when we're at the zoo, if she passes out from starvation not to count on me to carry her.

Well, guess what (again) . . . she said
she's not counting on me.

WHAT'S WRONG WITH THIS PICTURE?

Martha, in case you're interested (Mary
Ann is not), my tooth is very, very, very
loose. Pamela said she is sure it is coming
out soon. Joey offered again to yank it
out for me. But I told him I am going to
keep wiggling it and if it doesn't come out
on it's own, then I will think about what my

dentist calls, "An Extraction Plan."

We're at the zoo and here's what I'm wondering: Do animals get loose teeth? Is there a tooth fairy for animals? Is Mary Ann going to start acting like Mary Ann again?

Talk to you later.

Grrr! Mallory

AT THE ZOO

Dear Martha,

We've seen part of the zoo, but not all of it. There's a lot to see. We just stopped to get a drink of water, and I started wiggling my tooth, but as soon as I did, Mrs. Brooks flew over to where I was standing, grabbed my arm, and started screaming.

MRS. BROOKS, WHO DOES NOT LIKE DISEASES!

MRS. BROOKS: MALLORY MCDONALD, GET YOUR HANDS OUT OF YOUR MOUTH! THERE'S NO TELLING WHERE THEY'VE BEEN THIS MORNING AND THE LAST THING WE WANT IS FOR YOU TO GET SOME INFECTIOUS DISEASE.

When Mrs. Brooks stopped screaming, Pamela said her mom is kind of crazy when it comes to infectious diseases.

I told Mrs. Brooks that an infectious disease is the last thing I wanted to get too and that all I was trying to do was wiggle my loose tooth, but she said to wait and do it later when we take a bathroom break.

Arielle and Danielle asked when we are going to take a gift-store break. (There is a really big one here, and it looks like it sells a lot of cool stuff.) But Mr. Knight said we have a very full afternoon, which means no gift-store time.

OK. Water break is over.
G.2.G.C.T.R.O.T.Z. (Got 2 go C the rest of
the zoo.) Actually, what I really mean is
G.2.G.C.T.R.O.T.Z.W.A.P.B.M.I.B. (Got 2 go
C the rest of the zoo without a partner
because mine is busy.)
Mallory

STILL AT THE ZOO, BUT NOT FOR LONG

Dear Martha,

Mr. Knight said we have a few minutes left at the zoo, and then we are going museum hopping. (He didn't mean hopping like bunnies, he meant going from one museum to another.)

He said we have two assignments before we go. One is to write down what we thought was interesting about the zoo, and the other is to write a short letter to our favorite animal that we saw at the zoo. He said we should tell them about our experience at the zoo. Joey said he's going to write a letter to a lion, and Pamela is going to write her letter to an orangutan.

 That's a hint about my favorite animal, Mallory

Mallory McDonald's List of Interesting Things about the National Zoo

THING #1: There are lots of animals at this place. Over 2,400 of them to be exact. If I were an animal, I'd want to live here. There's always someone to play with or talk to (especially if your partner on a field trip isn't talking to you).

THING #2: If you come to the zoo, wear really comfortable (but still cute) shoes because you do a lot of walking. There's just so much to see here, including the monkey house, a tropical rain forest, lions, tigers, bears, elephants, birds, snakes, and even a dragon (the Komodo kind).

THING #3: There are some very big monkeys at the zoo called orangutans who know how to use a computer. HOW TOTALLY COOL IS THAT? Now, I bet you're starting to see why Pamela picked this as her favorite animal. I'm going to find out if they know how to do homework too, and if they do, I'm going to ask for an orangutan (which I'd like even more than

DO THEY SELL THESE AT THE TOY STORE?

a rotunda or chocolates on my pillow at night) for my next birthday.

THING #4: My favorite animal at the zoo is a panda bear named Tai Shan. His name means "peaceful morning." I like his name a lot, and I wish I was having one (a peaceful morning), which unfortunately, due to a certain someone whose first name starts with an "m," (I think you can guess who I mean), I am not.

THING #5: There are over 150 kinds of birds at the zoo. I know if Max were here, he'd say that including Mary Ann, who he calls Birdbrain, there are 151 kinds of birds. (Even though I hate when he calls her that, I think I'm starting to see why.)

OK. Now, my letter to my favorite animal.

Dear Tai Shan,

I've never written a letter to a panda, or any animal, except my cat Cheeseburger. But I'm glad I'm doing it because I could use someone to talk to.

We're supposed to be writing a letter about our experience at the zoo. Even though part of my experience (the seeing the animals part) was good, part of my experience (the sticking with your partner part) was not so good.

I tried sticking with my partner (Mary Ann), but she didn't try to stick with me at all. I don't know how much you know about partner sticking, but it is very hard to do when only one person is doing it.

Plus, it made me feel bad. I don't know if you have a best friend, but she's been mine since the day I was born. We've always done everything together, except now she's doing everything with somebody else and that somebody is a boy.

You look like a pretty sensitive little bear, so I'm sure you can understand why this kind of

M.N.B.F. short for MY NEW BEST FRIEND

(OK, really) hurts my feelings. Thanks so, so, so much for letting me talk to you. I feel better already.

By the way, the zookeeper told us that when you get a treat, you get apples, pears, and bamboo frozen in beet juice. I just want you to know that if you were my panda, I would make you a peanut butter and marshmallow sandwich. I think you would like that much better.

Big, huge hugs and kisses!

Mallory

A GIFT FROM ME TO YOU

P.S. In case you're wondering why I say things three times (like "Thanks so, so, so much"), it's because that's something Mary Ann and I made up . . . when we were still best friends.

P.P.S. My other best friend, Joey, made up a poem about you. I thought you might like to hear it.

There's a little bear at the National Zoo.
He's black and white, not black and blue.
His species name is the Giant Panda.
The only word that rhymes is Amanda.

I hope you liked his poem. And don't worry, I think when he grows up, he wants to be a skateboarder, not a poet.

BACK ON THE BUS

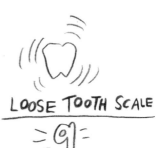

LOOSE TOOTH SCALE

Dear Martha,

Mr. Knight just told us to get back on the bus.

What we're doing: Eating our lunch on the way to the museums.

What we're not doing: Stopping at a bathroom for me to wiggle my loose tooth.

Mr. Knight told me we have a super busy schedule this afternoon, which does not include time for standing in front of a mirror wiggling a loose tooth (even though Pamela told him that my tooth is now a 9 on the loose tooth scale and that it wouldn't take much wiggling to come out).

Personally, I don't think it would take very long for me to stand in front of a mirror and wiggle my tooth. But we're already on the bus and Mr. Knight says

there's only one mirror on the bus and it's
for bus-driving not tooth-wiggling.
   See you at the museums!
   ☆ *Mallory*

M Is for Museums... and Missing!

AT THE SMITHSONIAN

Dear Martha,

We're at the Smithsonian Institution, which looks like a big castle. (C Postcard B Lo 2 C what I mean.)

It's actually not just one museum. It's 19 of them, and all together they have over 200 million things to see.

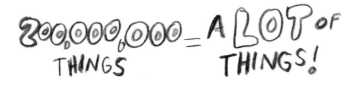

200,000,000 = A LOT OF
THINGS   THINGS!

Mr. Knight said we can't see them all in one afternoon, but we're going to see as many as we can. One other thing Mrs. Brooks just said is that some people say the Smithsonian, which is known as "The Castle," is haunted by ghosts.

When April heard that, she said she's glad we're staying at a hotel and not at the Smithsonian! I agree!

OK. We're off to see the museums!

☆ Mallory

BOO!

P.S. We're not off yet. Mr. Knight just gave us a *stick-with-your-partner-and-stay-with-the-group-while-we-tour-the-museums* speech. Now we're off!

STILL AT THE SMITHSONIAN, ABOUT TO GO TO THE MUSEUM OF AMERICAN HISTORY

Dear Martha,

Even though Mr. Knight just gave that speech, my partner is not sticking with me. (I bet you're so, so, so sick of hearing this because I'm so, so, so sick of writing it.)

I just went and found Mary Ann, who was talking to C-Lo. I told her chitchat time was up. I told her it was T.2.T. (time 2 tour). She came with me, but only after I said, "Let's go!" three times using my outdoor voice.

More later. We're off to the Museum of American History. It's filled with stuff from America's history. (I bet you guessed that from the name.)

☆ Mallory

IN THE LOBBY OF THE MUSEUM OF AMERICAN HISTORY

Dear Martha,

Mr. Knight said we have exactly 5 minutes. He says it is just enough time to write down a few things we saw here that we thought were interesting.

He says it's not enough time for me to go to the bathroom and pull my tooth out (which I know is pullable because Pamela said it looks like the only thing that's keeping it in my mouth is a little tiny piece of my gum).

☆ Mallory

P.S. If you're wondering if Mary Ann stayed with me while we were at the museum, you can stop wondering. Here's the answer: NO!

Mallory McDonald's List of Interesting Things about the Museum of American History

THING #1: This museum has tons of cool stuff in it, including George Washington's wooden teeth and Dorothy's ruby slippers from the *Wizard of Oz.* My official new favorite color is ruby. (It's probably Mary Ann's too, but I have no way of knowing, because I haven't spoken to her since we got here.)

THESE BELONG TO DOROTHY

THING #2: This museum has a nickname . . . America's Attic. The reason it got that name is because there's so much stuff from America's history shoved in this place, it seems like it's the official attic of our country. When C-Lo heard the nickname, he laughed and said, "That's a funny name for a museum." Then Mary Ann laughed and said, "I know, it's so funny." Personally, I don't think it's so funny.

THING #3: Even though I was having E.P.P (extreme partner problems), I loved a lot of stuff in this place (besides Dorothy's slippers).

My favorites were:

THE FIRST LADIES HALL. There are lots of dresses here that presidents' wives wore over the years. I think some of the presidents' wives could have used a little help from Fashion Fran, but they were still fun to see.

FRAN, HELP ME!

THE COLLECTION OF TEDDY BEARS. Some of the bears were over 100 years old, and I found out how they got their name. Teddy bears were named after President Theodore "Teddy" Roosevelt. One day he was out hunting and he refused to shoot a little bear cub. There was a cartoon about it in the newspaper, and after that, stuffed bears were called Teddy Bears. When we saw the bears, Mary Ann said to C-Lo, "Those bears are so, so, so cute!"

Martha, here's what
C-Lo said back to Mary
Ann (I hope I don't throw up
on you when I write this):
C-LO: Those bears are so,
 so, so cute, but not as
 cute as you.

THOMAS EDISON'S LIGHTBULB.
He invented the first one and Mrs. Brooks
said we should all be glad he did because
it would be a very dark world without
it. He also invented the telephone. I'm

glad he invented that
too, even though I'm
starting to wonder
if I still need a phone
since I'm not sure
if I still have a best
friend to call me.

STILL IN THE LOBBY OF THE MUSEUM OF AMERICAN HISTORY

Martha,

We're about to leave to go to museum #2 and I don't mean to keep bringing up the whole Mary-Ann-isn't-sticking-with-me-thing, but it's kind of the only thing on my mind (except for ruby slippers, teddy bears, and lightbulbs).

I think I wasted my wish at the beginning of the trip when I wished that it wouldn't be so bad living with Arielle and Danielle for four days. Living with them has been easy compared to being partners with Mary Ann.

I'm going to close my eyes and pretend like I'm at the wish pond on my street. I wish Mary Ann will stop acting like a GF and start acting like a BF.

TRANSLATION:
GF = girl friend   BF = Best Friend

I really hope my wish comes true.
☆ *Mallory*

P.S. Pamela just told me that her mom said the Museum of Natural History, where we're going next, is filled with really cool stuff and that it's really BIG. She said it's the size of 18 football fields. Wow! (If I had time, I'd write "Wow!" 18 times . . . one for each football field.)

AT THE MUSEUM OF NATURAL HISTORY

Dear Martha,

This museum was not as fun for me as the last museum.

It's not that they don't have cool stuff here. They do. But something bad happened. Actually, something really bad happened. I wish I didn't have to tell what it is, but you're probably really curious to know what that bad something is, so I'll tell you. But first, I have to use a 4-letter word.

L-O-S-T.

You heard right. The word is LOST, and that's what happened to me when my class was looking at the Hall of Bones. (It sounds like a scary place and trust me, it's even scarier if you get lost in it.)

But here's the thing: Getting LOST was not, I repeat, NOT my fault. It was someone else's fault and that someone's

BLAME HER!

name is Mary Ann. You're probably wondering how getting lost is her fault, so I'll tell you that too.

The Hall of Bones is filled with animal skeletons, which means lots of bones are there and teeth too. Seeing all those animal teeth made me start thinking about my own tooth, and particularly my loose tooth.

I could tell it was just about to fall out, and I didn't want to pull it out without looking, so I told Mary Ann that I was having a T.E. (tooth emergency), and I asked her if she would come with me to the bathroom to pull out my tooth.

Martha, you'll never believe what happened next. Mary Ann said *no,* that she wouldn't come with me. So I explained to her that partners are supposed to stick together at all times, and I asked her again and she said *no* again. I asked her a third time and guess what, she said *no* again!

So I had to go to the bathroom alone.

I ran into the last bathroom I saw (which didn't seem like it was too far away from where we were). I quickly pulled out my tooth, carefully wrapped it in a piece of toilet paper, and put it in my pocket.

NOTE TO TOOTH FAIRY: LOOK HERE

When I was done, I went right back to the Hall of Bones where my class was. But when I got there, my class wasn't.

They were gone! The only thing in the Hall of Bones were bones.

At first, I thought they had all gone to the bathroom, so I waited in the Hall of Bones for them to come back. But it didn't seem like they were coming back, so I decided to go look for them.

I went down one hallway, and I looked in a big room. What I did see: displays filled with alligators, frogs, turtles, and snakes. What I didn't see: my class.

So I went down another hallway, and I looked in another room that was filled with all kinds of bees, bugs, and butterflies in glass cases. But I still didn't see my class.

Then I went down another hallway, and another hallway, and another hallway. I'm not even sure what I saw because after a while all the hallways and the rooms started to look alike.

I looked everywhere, because all I wanted to do was find them. But Martha, what I found out is that in the Museum of Natural History (which is

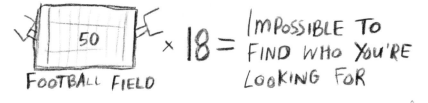

FOOTBALL FIELD $\times 18 =$ IMPOSSIBLE TO FIND WHO YOU'RE LOOKING FOR

definitely the size of 18 football fields), finding someone (even a whole class of someones) isn't easy to do.

I kept looking for a long time. (I'm not sure how long but it felt like a whole school year.) I even pretended like I was at the wish pond, and I made a wish that I would find them. But it didn't work. I couldn't find my class for a really long time, and that's when I got scared that I would never find them and that I would be stuck in the Museum of Natural History forever.

But then, a very official-looking guard found me and took me to my class.

Official-Looking Guard

Martha, that's bad, isn't it? Well, the story is about to get worse. When the guard took me to my class, I thought they would be happy to see me, but they weren't.

At first, Mr. Knight seemed like he was. But then he said he couldn't understand how I could wander off from the group after he had stressed how important it was to stay with the group and my partner.

I tried to explain that I just went to pull out my tooth. I even tried to show him my tooth.

Mr. Knight told me to put my tooth back in my pocket. Then he had a lot to say (none of it was about my tooth):

Mr. Knight: Mallory, I am extremely
    disappointed in you. We have a lot
    to talk about, but we can't do it right

now because we are on a very tight
schedule. But you and I are going to
have a long talk as soon as we get
back to the hotel.
And Mr. Knight wasn't the only one who
had something to say.

MAD FACES LOOKING AT ME

Mrs. Brooks said I almost gave her a heart attack.

Lots of kids in my class said that because of me, we barely had any time left to see Museum #3, which happens to be the Air and Space Museum and which also happens to be the one everyone was looking forward to the most.

Even Mary Ann didn't seem happy to see me. She didn't seem unhappy to see me either. It seemed like she couldn't decide if she was happy to see me or not.

Well, that's it. It's bad. It's also Mary Ann's fault. Don't you think? If she had stuck with me like a partner is supposed to do, none of this would have happened in the first place.

OK. Mr. Knight says we have to make our list of interesting things we saw before we leave for Museum #3.

It's kind of hard to make a list of interesting things when you just got lost and found and know that "getting in trouble" is right around the corner, but right now, I think I'd better do EVERYTHING Mr. Knight says.

☆ Mallory

Mallory McDonald's List of Interesting Things about the Museum of Natural History

THING #1: Right when you come into this place, you see a giant stuffed African bush elephant. What I learned about these elephants is not only that they are huge, but also that they run really fast. More than 25 miles an hour. When Mrs. Brooks told us that, Mr. Knight said, "You wouldn't want to do anything to get on this guy's bad side." Well, the good news is that my teacher is a regular man and not an African bush elephant.

THING #2: This place is the proud owner of the biggest blue diamond in the world. It's called the Hope Diamond. It's big and sparkly, and it reminded me of the wish pond on my street on a sunny day. If I had known I was going to get lost, I would have pretended like it was my wish pond and made a wish that I wouldn't get lost in this place.

That's it. *Mallory*

P.S. Mr. Knight said we're leaving to go to the Air and Space Museum. He said that we will love it and that it is one of the most popular spots in all of Washington, D.C., and that 8 million people visit it every year. I don't actually feel like going to another museum (ever), but I don't feel like I have a choice.

AT THE AIR AND SPACE MUSEUM

Dear Martha,

We just finished seeing the Air and Space Museum. I felt like every step I took was one step closer to getting in trouble. It was all anyone was talking about.

Read on to C what I mean.

Arielle: Someone's in trouble!

Danielle: Big trouble!

Joey: I hope you don't get in too much trouble.

Pamela: Mallory, you shouldn't have wandered off.

Then Pamela said I look older with my missing tooth. I know she was trying to make me feel better, but she didn't. I felt so bad, I didn't enjoy going through this museum . . . AT ALL.

While we were on the tour, Mary Ann said I seemed like I was in a bad mood, and she asked me if there was anything I wanted to talk about.

I said *no*. Then she asked me again and I said *no* again.

She asked me a third time (and she said it in a way that sounded like she wanted to talk too), but honestly, all of a sudden I didn't feel like talking to Mary Ann when she hasn't talked to me for practically the whole trip, so I said *no* again. Then Mary Ann didn't say anything else and neither did I.

But Mr. Knight did. He said to make our list of interesting things that we saw in the Air and Space Museum.

☹ *Mallory*

Mallory McDonald's List of Interesting Things about the Air and Space Museum

A Note to Mr. Knight: I was so upset about what happened at the last museum and even more upset thinking about the talk we're going to have when we get back to the hotel that I couldn't make a list of interesting things even though everyone (especially Joey) said there were tons of interesting plane and astronaut and rocket things to see here. I know you said 8,000,000 people visit this museum every year. Well, I hope that 7,999,999 had more fun than I did. Also,

just so you know, I couldn't enjoy the
freeze-dried "astronaut" ice
cream that everyone else
enjoyed. It's not that
it didn't taste good,
but when I ate it,
it made me wish
I could get in a
rocket and go far
away from here.
   I hope this
won't upset you to
hear this, Mr. Knight, but I'm not
actually looking forward to the talk we're
going to have when we get back to the
hotel. And unfortunately for me, you just
told everyone that it's time to get back
on the bus and go to the hotel. I guess
we'll be talking soon.
          Mallory

t.R.O.U.b.L.e

MALLORY McDONALD

PHOTO COURTESY OF PAMELA BROOKS

ANGRY TEACHER

NO WAY OUT

Tooth and Consequences

TIME GOES SLOWLY WHEN YOU'RE NOT HAVING FUN

Dear Martha,

I had my "talk" with Mr. Knight. It started out REALLY bad and lasted for a REALLY long time.

Here's what happened.

Right when we got back to the hotel, Mr. Knight said that everybody could go to their rooms except for Mallory McDonald. (That's me, in case you weren't sure.)

Then he said for me to please come with him to the coffee shop. Martha, what I learned about coffee shops is that they are much more fun to go to in the morning when they are filled with people drinking coffee than they are in the afternoon when they are practically empty except for mad teachers and students who are about to get in trouble.

When we got to the coffee shop, Mr. Knight told me to sit down, that he wanted to talk to me. I told him if he wanted to order some coffee, we could wait and talk after he finished his coffee.

DRINK ME

But unfortunately, Mr. Knight wasn't in the mood to drink coffee. He was in the mood to talk, and here's what he had to say.

If you have to go to the bathroom, now is a good time because Mr. Knight had a <u>lot</u> to say.

IMPORTANT ANNOUNCEMENT: CONVERSATION WITH MR. KNIGHT IN THE COFFEE SHOP

MR. KNIGHT: (talking in a mad voice) Mallory, what happened today was very serious. I set the rules for this field trip, and I reiterated them many times. You were supposed to stay with the group and your partner at all times. These rules were set for your safety. You didn't follow them, and as a result, you were separated from the group. Fortunately, nothing bad happened to you, but something could have. Not only did you disobey me and endanger yourself by not following the rules, but you also wasted many people's time. We spent a long time looking for you, and as a result, our class had very little time at the Air and Space Museum. Coming on this field trip was a tremendous privilege for our class. I expected exemplary behavior, and you did not display that.

Mallory: Can you please tell me what exemplary means?

This would come in handy

Mr. Knight: Exemplary means excellent, and that is the kind of behavior I expected from you. Unfortunately, it is not what I got. Mallory, I am very disappointed in you.

(pausing) What do you have to say for yourself?

Mallory: Mr. Knight, I'm really sorry I didn't follow your rules. I didn't mean to get separated from the group. I just went to the bathroom for a second to pull out my tooth, and when I came back, everyone was gone.

Mr. Knight: (looking like explanation still doesn't make it right) Mallory, why didn't you ask permission to go to the bathroom?

Mallory: (hanging head, not saying anything)

Mr. Knight: (crossing arms across his chest) Mallory, I'm waiting for an explanation. You shouldn't have left the group. You were supposed to stick with your partner.

Mallory: I tried to stick with my partner,

but my partner didn't want to stick with me. Mary Ann was my partner, but the whole trip she acted like C-Lo was her partner.

Mr. Knight: (listening, not saying anything)

Mallory: (continuing, telling Mr. Knight everything that happened on the trip with Mary Ann, and how Mary Ann spent most of her time being C-Lo's girlfriend and not her partner) I'm supposed to be Mary Ann's best friend, but I think she cares more about some stupid boy than she cares about me.

WHAT MY TEACHER LOOKS LIKE WHEN HE'S WAITING.

END OF REALLY BAD PART OF CONVERSATION WITH MR. KNIGHT

NOTE TO MARTHA: Here's where the REALLY BAD part of the conversation ends. I think it would have kept being really bad, because I know Mr. Knight, and I know he had a lot more to say, except that something really surprising happened. There's no way you will guess what it is, so I'm just going to tell you. Are you ready? Here it is...

MARY ANN WALKED INTO THE COFFEE SHOP!

I know, you think you're hearing things, but you're not. Mary Ann came over to the booth where I was sitting with Mr. Knight and

LIFE IS FULL OF SURPRISES!

said she had some things she would like to say to him and to me.

Mary Ann: (talking to Mr. Knight) Mr. Knight, I know you're mad at Mallory for getting lost, but I just want to say that what happened wasn't totally Mallory's fault. I mean, I guess she shouldn't have gone to the bathroom without asking permission. But I wasn't a very good partner. I didn't stick with her when I was supposed to.

Mary Ann: (talking to Mallory) I'm sorry I wasn't a good partner or a good best friend on this trip. I don't blame you for being upset. If I were you, I'd be upset too. I was so busy thinking about how I was feeling, I didn't think about how you were feeling.

Mallory: I'm not sure what to say.

Mr. Knight: (clearing throat) I know what I want to say, and I want you both to listen. I don't think either of you exhibited exemplary behavior on this trip.

Mary Ann: Can you please tell me what *exemplary* means?

(Mallory explaining to Mary Ann what *exemplary* means)

Mr. Knight: (continuing) Mallory, you should have followed the rules. No matter what other people do, it is always your responsibility to follow my rules. Mary Ann, no matter what is going on in your life, you should always try to be a kind and considerate friend. I think as you girls can see, rules are meant to be followed, and friendships, even the best of them, aren't always perfect. Sometimes things happen, and when they do, it is important to tell each other how you are feeling. Do you understand?

(Both girls nodding)

Mr. Knight: And as for your punishment . . .

Mary Ann: (looping her arm through
   Mallory's) Mr. Knight, if you're going
   to punish Mallory, you have to punish
   me too.

We're a package deal!

Mr. Knight: (smiling) I think you've both
   learned an important lesson and been
   through a lot today. We're on a field
   trip and field trips are supposed to
   be fun, so if it's OK with you girls, why

don't we save the punishment for
another time?

(Mallory and Mary Ann jumping around
the coffee shop hugging each other and
screaming!)

END OF CONVERSATION WITH MR. KNIGHT (AND MARY ANN) IN THE COFFEE SHOP

STILL IN HOTEL, IN ROOM, JUST FINISHED ANOTHER TALK, THIS TIME WITH MARY ANN

Dear Martha,

You probably think I spend a lot of
time talking to people, and I guess today
I have. But after I left the coffee shop
with Mary Ann, we came back to our
room. At first, we didn't say anything
to each other. But then, Mary Ann said

she had some things she wanted to say to me.

CONVERSATION WITH MARY ANN IN THE HOTEL ROOM, ACTUALLY IN THE HOTEL ROOM BATHROOM BECAUSE ARIELLE AND DANIELLE WERE IN THE HOTEL ROOM AND THEY SAID THEY COULDN'T HEAR THE TV WITH ALL THE YAKKING GOING ON

Mary Ann: Mallory, I really I hope you'll forgive me. I know I haven't been a very good friend on this trip, and I feel really badly about it.

Who's Counting?!?

Mallory: It just seems like you spent a LOT of your time on

the trip with C-Lo and just a LITTLE bit of time with me.

Mary Ann: I didn't mean to spend just a little bit of time with you. The thing is, it didn't feel like I was spending a lot of time with C-Lo.

Mallory: I don't get it.

Mary Ann: It's kind of like when we have a sleepover. If I come over on Friday, before we know it, it's Saturday night. We've had so much fun being together, we don't even realize a whole day has gone by.

Mallory (what I was thinking): How can spending time with C-Lo be as much fun as spending time with me?

Mallory (what I said): OK. So I guess I get it. You like C-Lo. But can't you have a boyfriend and a best friend at the same time?

BF #1   BF #2

WHO WOULD YOU CHOOSE?

Mary Ann: (throwing her arms around
   me and hugging me SUPER tight) Of
   course, I can do both things at the
   same time. We only have one day
   of the trip left, but you're my best,
   best, best friend and a whole lot more
   important to me than any boyfriend,
   and I promise that starting right now,
   I'll be the world's best, best, best
   friend and partner.

Danielle: (opening bathroom door) You two should get out here right now, the movie is about to start.

Mallory: (sticking her arm through Mary Ann's) Want to go watch the movie?

Mary Ann: I can't think of anything I'd rather do.

END OF CONVERSATION WITH MARY ANN IN BATHROOM

WHY IS WATCHING A MOVIE IN A HOTEL EVEN MORE FUN THAN WATCHING ONE AT HOME?

A NOTE TO MR. KNIGHT:

 I hope you don't mind that I wrote about our conversation in the coffee shop in my travel journal. Even though it started off pretty bad, it ended on a happy note.

Plus, I've told Martha just about everything that's happened on this trip, so I kind of couldn't leave that part out.

And here's the most important part of all: Thanks for not punishing anybody on a field trip. I think you made a good decision.

Sincerely,

Mallory (and Mary Ann, who is sitting next to me while I write this)

P.S. These best friends think their teacher is super cool. Mr. Knight, that means you.

B.F.F.! (Best Friends Forever!)

M Is for Money

AT THE HOTEL, BUT NOT FOR LONG

Dear Martha,

After yesterday, I didn't think I'd ever feel like going anywhere else that started with an "M," but this morning (which is our last morning, because we leave Washington, D.C., this afternoon, BOO HOO!) we're going to a place called the Money Factory.

It's not really a money factory (well, it sort of is). We're going to the United States Bureau of Engraving and Printing, otherwise known as the Money Factory, and Mr. Knight said it's where money gets printed.

After we see the Bureau of

Printing and Engraving, Mr. Knight says we're going to do one last thing before we head home, and that thing is shopping. OK. I'm going to pretend like I'm at the wish pond on my street, close my eyes, and make a wish. I wish the people at the Money Factory will give me some of the money they print so I can use it when we go shopping.

I just told Mary Ann my wish and she said she wishes for the same thing.

Time to stop writing and wishing. Mrs. Brooks just said it's time to get on the bus and off we go!

$ Mallory

AT THE MONEY FACTORY (IN THE BATHROOM)

Martha,
We're at the Money Factory and I

have some good news! Unlike the White
House, you CAN use the bathroom in this
place, which is great because right when
we got here that's exactly what I had to
do. And so did April, Dawn, Pamela, Mary
Ann, and Zoe.

Our tour is about to start, so T.T.Y.L.
(talk to you later).

$ Mallory

STILL AT THE MONEY FACTORY

Dear Martha,

We just finished our tour, and everybody in my class agreed that it was SO, SO, SO COOL! We got to see money being printed. I've never seen so much money in my life!

Mr. Knight said it's time to spend a few minutes writing down what we found interesting about this place. It won't be hard at all for me because I thought just about everything about this place was interesting.

$ Mallory

Mallory McDonald's List of Interesting Things about the United States Bureau of Engraving and Printing

THING #1: You have to go through security to get inside. I think they make you do that because they don't want anyone to steal the money.

THING #2: When you walk inside the Bureau of Engraving and Printing, the first thing you see is one million dollars! DON'T FAINT! I almost did when I

saw it. There's a big stack of $20 bills that equals $1,000,000, and I'm not kidding when I tell you it's a lot of $20s.

THING #3: Money isn't made out of paper. It's made out of cloth. Cotton and linen, to be exact. Mary Ann and I decided we're going to write to Fashion Fran and tell her, so maybe she'll do a TV show about clothes made out of money and maybe she'll let us model in it since it was our idea in the first place.

THING #4: The Money Factory prints over $600 million a day. Even though Joey never says things three times, when he heard that, he said, "That is so, so, so much money!"

THING #5: The Money Factory smells. If you're wondering what

BLACK
INK
+
GREEN
INK
= P.U.!

it smells like, I'll tell you. It smells like ink, the black and green kind, because that's what they use to print the money with.

At the end of the tour, we all got to stop in a photo booth to have our picture printed on a $20 bill.

Mr. Knight says it's time to get back on the bus. If you ask me, the Money Factory was very cool, but Mary Ann says no more cool than where we're going next!

$ Mallory

Shop Here!

Mary Ann and me with Virginia

Bye Bye, boo Hoo!

Souvenirs

ON THE BUS

Dear Martha,

Mr. Knight just announced that our trip is not officially over, but it almost is. He said we have one last stop to make before we head home. He said that we're going to a very large memorabilia store and that it's the perfect place to buy gifts for other people or souvenirs for ourselves.

Mrs. Brooks said she wanted to add that the word *souvenir* comes from the French verb *souvenir*, which means to remember. She said that the reason you buy souvenirs is to remember your trip. She also said we only have 15 minutes to shop so we better make it snappy.

OK. We're here! Mr. Knight wasn't kidding when he said this store is big. It's even called The World's Biggest Souvenir Store.

C.U.A.I.S. (That's short for C U after I shop!)

Souvenir me! That means "remember me" in French (I think).

🛍 *Mallory*

BACK ON THE BUS

Dear Martha,

We just finished shopping and got back on the bus. The World's Biggest Souvenir Store is a really fun place.

Right when we got there, a lady named Virginia (I wonder if she's from Virginia and that's why her parents named her that) gave us all little American flags and said, "Welcome to The World's Biggest

Souvenir Store!" Then she told us there are lots of things to buy inside and to take our time and enjoy it.

We had only 15 minutes to enjoy it, but everybody bought a lot of stuff. I bet you're wondering what I bought, so I won't keep you in suspense any longer.

I bought Mom and Dad matching  coffee mugs with a picture of the White House on them. I also got one for Mrs. Brooks because I  know she likes coffee.

I bought Cheeseburger a  new collar with stars and stripes on it.

I bought Max a really nice present since he let me bring his iPod.

I got him a back scratcher that looks like the Washington Monument with a fork on the end of it. If he doesn't want to use it for his back, Virginia told me he can also use it for his dinner.

I got something for Mr. Knight too. I'm going to surprise him. I just want him to know that I think it was really great of him to bring us to Washington.

And last, but not least, I got myself something. I bought a snow globe with the White House in it. Joey and Pamela bought one too. Joey said that when you shake it, it looks like the White House is stuck in a snowstorm.

And guess what... somebody else

Tooth holder

bought something for me and that somebody is Mary Ann. Right when we got on the bus, she gave me a red, white, and blue little, tiny tooth holder.

When she gave it to me, she said she just wanted me to know that I would always be her best, best, best friend and that she was really sorry about everything that happened. She also said this would make it very easy for the Tooth Fairy to find my tooth.

When Arielle and Danielle saw it, they said it was totally stupid to believe in the Tooth Fairy, but Mary Ann told them what her mom and my mom have always said about the Tooth Fairy. *Those who believe, receive.*

I told Mary Ann that I love, love, love the tooth holder, even more than I love the snow globe (which I love a lot).

Then she said that she picked the red, white, and blue tooth holder because after this trip, we will always be red, white, and true blue best friends. To tell you the truth, I think she picked the red, white, and blue box because red, white, and blue is the only color they sell here.

But I told her that when I get home, I'm going to put my tooth in it and put it under my pillow and that I think the tooth fairy will love it as much as I do.

OK, Martha. The bus is starting to roll away and we're on our way home. It seems like we just got here and it's already time to leave. Even though there were some times on the trip that I wish could have been different, we learned so much and had so much fun. Everyone says they're sad the trip is over, and I am too.

Arielle and Danielle say they will miss sleeping in a hotel.

Boo Hoo!

Mary Ann says she will miss getting to wear our matching flag pajamas.

Pamela said she will miss all of the cool places we visited.

Mrs. Brooks says she will miss getting to fill people in on important facts about important places. (I'm not sure anybody else will miss this.)

And C-Lo says he will miss learning about all of the important buildings and documents and people that are part of America's history. (Personally, I don't know how much C-Lo learned on this trip. He was pretty busy doing other things while he was supposed to be learning.)

But he also said he can't believe his first field trip in this country has come to an end. And neither can I. We waited for such a long time to go, and it feels like it went by so quickly.

Mary Ann asked him if he ever got to take field trips in Mexico, and he said he took a really fun one to a place called Acapulco, which is a beach town.

When he said that, I told Mr. Knight that we should go there next. Mr. Knight laughed. He said Washington, D.C., is all the field trip we get.

So I guess that's it. It's time to say, "Good-bye, Washington, D.C.!" I will *souvenir* you forever. That's French for, "I'll never forget this trip. Not ever!"

And Martha, I won't forget you either. You've been an exemplary (that means excellent, in case you forgot) travel journal.

Thanks for listening to everything I had to say.

♡ instead of a ☆ and it's red, white, and true blue!

Mallory

Home, Sweet Home!

AT HOME, ON MY BED, WITH MY CAT, CHEESEBURGER

Dear Martha,

I got home this afternoon and even though I didn't think I wanted our trip to end, I'm really glad to be here. I've learned lots of things about coming home from a field trip, and I thought I'd share them with you.

Mallory McDonald's List of Interesting Things about Being Home

THING #1: People like when you bring them presents. Mom and Dad and Max all liked what I brought them. Max used the back scratcher tonight to eat his macaroni and cheese. When I told him what it was for, he said he thought it was a giant fork.

THING #2: Food at home tastes better than food on a field trip. Even though I didn't actually get to taste much of the food on our field trip, I can tell that the food Mom makes at home tastes a lot better than just about everything we ate in Washington (except for the apple pie, which tasted great).

THING #3: Even though it is fun being in a hotel, it's a whole lot more fun being in my own room with my cat, Cheeseburger.

THING #4: You are tired when you come home from a field trip. And that is why I'm going to stop writing, turn off my light, and go to sleep.

☾☆ Nighty Nite! Mallory

A Letter from Mallory

Dear Mr. Knight,

I can't believe we're already back from Washington, D.C. Thank you so, so, so much for taking us. I will always remember it (and not just because you made us write down all of those interesting facts).

Several items are enclosed in this envelope:

Item #1: My travel journal. It was blank when we left, and now it's all filled up. (And most of what I had to write about was good.)

Item #2: A Trip Report Card. I know you didn't ask for one, but I'm giving you an A+ in every category.

Item #3: A special surprise for you! I bought these flag socks for you at the Souvenir Shop. If you wear them 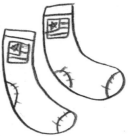 with your flag tie, you can be patriotic from your neck down to your feet. I really hope you like them.

T.A.F.T.U. (that's short for thanks again for taking us).

MR. KNIGHT'S REPORT CARD

REPORT CARD
GRADE:
A+

I hope you had as much fun in Washington as I did!

Sincerely,

Mallory McDonald

A Special Scrapbook

Mary Ann came over Saturday night for a scrapbooking sleepover. We made our Washington scrapbook, wore our flag pajamas, and pretended like we were sleeping at a hotel.

It was a little hard to do without those little bottles of shampoo and conditioner and the American flag chocolates, but we put up a sign in my room that said, "The Mallory Suite."

When we were done with our scrapbook, we gave Mom, Dad, and Cheeseburger a photo show.

These were some of their favorites.

This one is of me, Mary Ann, Joey, and C-Lo on the bus. I don't think it is a very good picture of me (I had just eaten three doughnuts, all on the right side of my mouth), but Mom, Dad, and Mary Ann all thought it was cute. Even Cheeseburger purred when she saw it.

This one is of all the girls on the steps of the Capitol. Mom said she liked this picture because it has a very patriotic, happy feel to it.

Here's one of Mr. Knight and me. Mom says that even though Mr. Knight and I have had our ups and downs, she thinks I'm lucky to have him as a teacher this year. And I think Mom is right. I'm really learning a lot.

This one was taken in front of the souvenir shop. Dad said he liked this picture the best, and he also liked how Mary Ann and I glued our flags together on the front of our scrapbook.

Dad said that seeing the flags reminds him of Mary Ann and me. He says he likes seeing us together. And the truth is . . . I do too. I guess best friends, even lifelong ones, don't see eye to eye (or tooth to tooth) on everything. As Mr. Knight said, friendships aren't always perfect, but I think my friendship with Mary Ann is really, really, really good. No, scratch that, I think it is really, really, really great. Especially when we get to do fun stuff like go to Washington, D.C.

There's no telling where we'll be going or what we'll be doing in the future, but one thing is for sure, as long as Mary Ann and I will be doing it together, I know it will be fun.

Au revoir (Mrs. Brooks taught us this phrase as we were getting off the bus. She said it means good-bye in French).

So good-bye for now.

Big, huge hugs and kisses,

Mallory

Carolrhoda Books
A division of Lerner Publishing Group, Inc.
241 First Avenue North
Minneapolis, MN 55401 U.S.A.

Website address: www.lernerbooks.com

Library of Congress Cataloging-in-Publication Data

Friedman, Laurie B.
        Red, white & true blue Mallory / by Laurie Friedman ; illustrations by Jennifer
Kalis.
            p.   cm.
        Summary: Mallory's journal of her fourth-grade trip to Washington, D.C. reveals
how much fun she has, despite a loose tooth, being upset with her best friend,
Mary Ann, and getting separated from her class in a museum.
        ISBN: 978-0-8225-8882-5 (trade hard cover : alk. paper)
        1. Washington (D.C.)—Juvenile fiction. [1. Washington (D.C.)—Fiction.
2. School field trips—Fiction. 3. Tourism—Fiction. 4. Best friends—Fiction.
5. Friendship—Fiction. 6. Diaries—Fiction.] I. Kalis, Jennifer, ill. II. Title.
PZ7.F89773Red 2009
[Fic]—dc22   2008016035

Manufactured in the United States of America
5 — BP — 3/1/10